JEFF & MIKE'S
MAN CAVE
AUTHORIZED PERSONNEL ONLY

BRING
YOUR
OWN
BEER

THE
GAME'S
ALWAYS
ON!

The Man Cave Book

The Man Cave Book

Mike Yost & Jeff Wilser

HARPER

My wife says
I never listen
to her.
At least I think
that's what
she said.

HARPER

THE MAN CAVE BOOK. Copyright © 2011 by Michael H. Yost and Jeff Wilser.
All rights reserved. Printed in the United States of America. No part
of this book may be used or reproduced in any manner whatsoever
without written permission except in the case of brief quotations
embodied in critical articles and reviews. For information address
HarperCollins Publishers, 10 East 53rd Street, New York, NY 10022.

HarperCollins books may be purchased for educational, business,
or sales promotional use. For information please write:
Special Markets Department, HarperCollins Publishers,
10 East 53rd Street, New York, NY 10022.

FIRST EDITION

Designed by Timothy Shaner, nightanddaydesign.biz

Library of Congress Cataloging-in-Publication Data
is available upon request.

ISBN 978-0-06-200392-8

11 12 13 14 15   OV/RRD   10 9 8 7 6 5 4 3 2 1

Behind every man is his man cave.

Behind every man cave is a story. This book tells that story. The inspiration, the joy, the hardwired wisdom. It's all here. We clear up misconceptions, spread the gospel, and lay down the rules and regulations. You'll find tips for rookies, rewards for veterans, and, hopefully, the answer to the great question: "What were you thinking?"

The Man Cave Book focuses on what makes a great man cave great. Why are they built? How are they built? What can we learn about our own caves, our culture, our humanity, and our own souls?

Along the journey, we guarantee plenty of surprises, many laughs, and, if men were permitted to cry, a few tears of happiness.

A man cave can be anything: a stylish lounge, a home theater, a high-tech Mecca to gaming, a music studio, or just an ode to your once great college crash-pad. The world is your oyster. Even the International Space Station is getting a man cave.

There are many excellent reasons to build a man cave. It's easier, cheaper, and safer than going to a bar. It's a harmless outlet. It rekindles friendships. It keeps your trash from the rest of the house. It can even help spark a relationship, especially your relationship with Jack, Johnnie, and Bud.

The man cave is an opportunity—maybe our best and last opportunity— for freedom. Freedom from responsibility, freedom from work, and freedom from taste.

When single, we let our walls go bare. When married, we let our walls go pink. And something happens to us when we settle into domesticity. After the wedding, we swallow our egos, phase out our buddies, and choke back tears as our homes—our very *homes*—collect bizarre items like gravy boats, potpourri, and vacuum cleaners.

We sacrifice. We stamp out our past. We even throw out the essentials, those must-have objects like the Redskins couch with built-in beer holders, the wall-sized tapestry of Cloud City, the original Atari that no longer works, the stuffed heads of falcons, and the semi-automatic, 800-rounds-per-minute assault rifles that are probably legal in at least three states. We scrap all of this. And like Parisians in the early 1940s, we endure.

But something's not right. We feel a rumbling deep in our bellies, a primordial urge, a sense that we've lost a shred of our identity. Lesser men will feed this hunger with mistresses, alcoholism, a midlife crisis.

Not us. We're stronger. But we wonder . . . *what if.*

What if there's a way to have it all? What if there's a way to resurrect the glory of our past, to cherish our hobbies, and to create a sanctuary—a magical getaway—that lets us nourish our souls, with dignity, and without disrupting our families?

Enter THE MAN CAVE.

The 7 Constructions of a Man Cave

The meat and potatoes. These are the blue-collar caves, the functional caves, the triumphant intersection of comfort, simplicity, and hard-won goodies. The bulk of man caves (especially ones not featured in this book) will fall into this category—take a look at Mark Lau's on page 8.

The goal is to accumulate more of one type of item than anyone else in the world. It doesn't matter what that item is. It matters that you have at least 10,000 of them. And they can be tasteful, too: just look at the shrine to Coca-Cola by Wade Miller, page 24.

Sports aren't just watched here. They're played. You rig your cave to accommodate the toughest athletic challenges known to man: pool, poker, shuffleboard, and the Xbox. Of course, it's also the ideal venue for watching the game—just ask Jim Meehan, owner of a replica stadium, page 51.

In the Beginning

The Inspiration: ManCaveSite.org

Man caves begin and end with Mike Yost. He is the uncontested king. The guts, soul, and spirit of the man cave and much of this book come from Mike's website, ManCaveSite.org. Mike Yost is the man. He started the online community, he grew the site, and his thoughts are stamped in this book's DNA. It is the brave men of that community who have graciously shared their caves, dreams, obsessions, and do-it-yourself gone wild and inspiring stories in this book. My role is researcher, interviewer, writer. In other words, if you think something is a good idea, it belongs to Mike and the ManCaveSite community. If you think it makes no sense, chalk it up to me.

–Jeff Wilser

Man Cave 1.0

You are looking at history. This is the cave of Marty Peterson, a good friend of Mike Yost. Without Marty's cave, ManCaveSite.org wouldn't exist, this book wouldn't exist, and, quite probably, Western civilization as we know it would not exist. When our descendants find Marty's cave in ten thousand years, they will be setting foot among the mammoth-painters of our time.

In 2008, I had a buddy who built a man cave (Marty Peterson). I'd never heard the term before. He made it from an RV garage. We'd hang out there and have a great time. He put so much effort into this thing, and I wanted to showcase his work. I checked the Internet, looking for a central place to show it off . . . nothing.

So I had the idea to build a site that's free, that lets men showcase their man caves, and that provides resources.

If you plan to build a man cave, make it your own. Every man cave is a reflection of its owner's personality. That's what's so neat. Everyone is different. Some guys ask me, "What should be in there?" Build it to make *you* happy.

It's always an ongoing effort. It's never done. Every guy who owns a man cave will tell you it's always a work in progress. They're always finding stuff in flea markets, on eBay; that's part of the fun.

The "Men Only" concept is a misconception. People think that it's some women-hater club.

Couldn't be any further from the truth. And every man cave owner that *I* talk to is among the most devoted fathers you will find. Family first. And that's another nice thing about the man cave: it's at home. The man is there.

Once you finish the book be sure to join the man cave community at ManCaveSite.org. You'll find thousands more photos and resources, links, message forums, and other fellow cave dwellers.

—Mike Yost

Origins of the Man Cave: The Boyhood Fort

Nothing really changes in life. Except that we gain weight, lose hair, piss more, read less, and, if we're honest, occasionally lose interest in sex. Besides all *that*, nothing really changes in life. The man cave is simply an updated version of the tree house, or the boyhood fort.

	Boyhood Fort	Man Cave
Who's allowed	Not girls–they have cooties	Not women–they have authority
Primary materials used in construction	Wood, stuff your mom doesn't want	Particleboard, stuff your wife doesn't want
Key activities inside	Goofing around, avoiding responsibility	Goofing around, avoiding responsibility
Peak periods of use	After school, weekends	After work, weekends
What other family members think of the space	Patient, not thrilled, but it's better to just roll with the program and hope for the best	Patient, not thrilled, but it's better to just roll with the program and hope for the best
Slumber parties with buddies?	Yes	No
Reason that your bedroom, living room, and house will not suffice for leisure space	"Huh? It's a *tree house*, you dork."	"Huh? It's a *man cave*, you douche."
Food and beverages consumed	Soda and unhealthy snacks	Beer and unhealthy snacks
Masturbating inside?	When old enough	When young enough
Spend the night inside?	Not as a habit, but it's been known to happen	Not as a habit, but it's been known to happen
Stuff on walls	Posters, sports memorabilia	Posters, sports memorabilia
Money spent on space	As little as possible	As much as possible
Is this a phase you will outgrow?	Yes	No

The Everyman (Basic) Cave

1

No muss, no fuss. These caves show that everybody—yes, even you—can make a man cave without plundering your savings, gutting your home, or ditching your family. All it takes is a little space and a little creativity—and a lot of beer.

America's First Man Cave: Monticello

Thomas Jefferson was a busy man. He wrote a letter of some import, he invented the swivel chair, he ran a farm, he ran a country, he found time to slander his old buddy John Adams, and, perhaps most important, he created the first man cave.

How else can we describe Monticello? Consider. Without the influence of any woman, Jefferson, a widower, kept tinkering and tinkering, stuffing it with collectibles that he schlepped from Paris.

He designed it. He filled it with gadgets. He obsessed over it. Hell, even when he was *president*, he wrote letters about his improvements for Monticello. The man just couldn't stop and say *Enough*. If Jefferson were alive today, he would be that CEO in the top floor office, delaying meetings, dodging email, wasting time in Photoshop designing a new bathroom for his cave.

Bobby Schaff

The Man Cave Book: *Nice garage.*

Bobby Schaff: I'm actually sitting in here right now, watching the LSU game.

You're an LSU fan? Never would have guessed.

It was my wife's idea. It was the best idea she's ever come up with. We had a game room in Texas, but then when we moved back to Louisiana, there wasn't room for all my stuff. I was going to sell the pool table, and my wife said, "Why not put it in the garage?"

Do you use the garage for anything else, like, a car?

No. Not at all. There's no room. I got an outdoor storage space and moved everything else out—tools, lawn equipment—so now the garage is just the LSU man cave.

Do all the neighbors come over to hang?

If you build it, they will come. It's kind of become a neighborhood watering hole.

Is the man cave only for men?

In the beginning, it was a lot of guys always coming over, and there was this stigma of the women saying, "Oh no, they're all going over to Bobby's house again, drinking and cutting up." Eventually I told everyone to bring their wives, and now it's not just guys, it's women and the kids. **It's not just a man cave, it's a family cave.**

Did you do all this yourself?

No. I'm not a real handy person. But I have some neighbors that are. And a lot of the stuff I ended up doing, like converting the refrigerator to a keg-o-rator, is from the help of neighbors. They're the skilled laborers, and I'm just handing out the tools. It became a neighborhood project.

Why do you like having a man cave?

You're leaving behind that lifestyle of being single and hanging out in bars. You don't have time for that stuff any more, so this is a release, this keeps my sanity.

Any advice for others?

Marry the right person. If you're not married to the right person, you can't do any of this.

COMMON MISCONCEPTIONS

IT'S ONLY FOR MEN. The man cave should be *originated* by men, *driven* by men, and *built* by men. But the other gender can visit. A subtle yet critical distinction.

IT MUST BE TACKY. People think that 100 percent of man caves must, by definition, be decorated with beer cans, neon signs, and duct tape as the coup de grace. False. That's only true 99 percent of the time.

IT'S ISOLATING. They can be. But most (not all) owners use the room as a temporary getaway, not a permanent hideaway. All relationships need space. This is simply healthy breathing space, even if, yes, the breath smells like beef jerky.

IT'S EXPENSIVE. A man cave is like a garden—it's only as expensive as you make it. Like a garden, it grows things (mold, useless collections, mooching neighbors). Unlike a garden, it doesn't suck.

IT'S BAD FOR A MARRIAGE. The trick is being honest and upfront about why you want the cave, how long you'll be in there, and that she's welcome, sometimes.

IT'S FILLED WITH BEER. If a man cave were filled with beer, there would be no room left for the rest of life's treasures—bourbon, rum, and tequila.

MARK LAU

> **I'M A BIG FAN OF INDY,** and my fiftieth birthday party was an adventure theme. So I dressed up like Indy, we decorated the whole house with jungle/treasure stuff, and even had a cake that looked like a treasure chest. ▪ I'd like to dress like Indy all the time—very comfortable—but people might think

it a bit strange, or ask me if I'm a lion-tamer or something. ▪ THE THEME OF MY CAVE IS 'ME.' I ONLY HAVE STUFF IN THERE THAT INTERESTS ME. Even the roll of John Wayne toilet paper in the bathroom speaks of me, 'It's rough, it's tough, and it doesn't take crap off of anybody.' ▪ THE COLLECTION OF SWORDS DEPICTS MY LOVE OF MY GERMAN HERITAGE, MY LOVE OF AMERICA, AND MY LOVE OF WEAPONS. ▪ The American flag is one we used to fly at the house I grew up in Torrance, California. It's only a forty-eight-star, since my folks got it before Alaska and Hawaii were brought into the Union. *"*

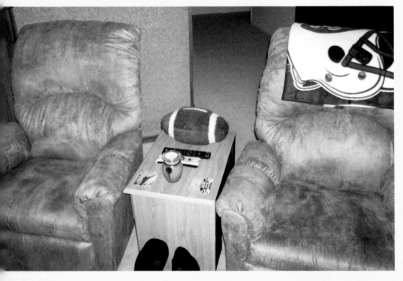

For a man to be comfortable in his own skin, he needs to be comfortable in his own cave. **HE NEEDS A COUCH**. A big one. A comfy one. If it can be described as a "love seat," it should be doused with kerosene and lit with a match.

RICHARD DIXON

BUILDER AWARD

"THE KIDS IN THE NEIGHBORHOOD, AND MY NEPHEWS, LOVE TO COME VISIT AND HEAR MY EXAGGERATED STORIES, BOTH TRUE AND FALSE. The Cape Buffalo mount required a fifteen-mile walk in over 100-degree heat in Zambia. *Motivation for building cave: A place where I could hide from my wife* "

CAVE ESSENTIALS

TELEVISION Thousands of people work very, very hard to create, produce, and broadcast TV shows. Do your part. Watch.

SOFA Function should trump form. Comfort matters. If it's not possible to sleep on it for at least three hours, you've done something wrong.

FRIDGE Theoretically, you could walk to the kitchen every time you need a beer. Theoretically, you could call an ambulance every time you stub your toe. Screw theory: embrace self-reliance.

SPACE You shouldn't feel smothered. Get plenty of space. It is a cave, but it should feel like a castle.

SPORTS MEMORABILIA Banners. Hats. Old plastic cups. Quantity, quantity, quantity. Your goal is this: if your childhood sports hero—the one you have on your wall—were to actually *enter your cave*, he would freak out, run away, and think about calling the authorities.

ALCOHOL A man cave without booze is like cereal without milk. The two go hand in hand. Drink responsibly. (And since you're not driving anywhere, you're off to a good start.)

STEREO Music nurtures the soul, invigorates the spirit, excites the mind, and covers up the sounds of your farts.

Millions of men are unfamiliar with this concept. So we'll start with the basics. *Table. Noun. A hard flat surface, usually supported by four legs, that's used for eating meals.*

IT'S A HELL OF AN INVENTION. For 99.9999999 percent of men, when left to our own devices, we eat on the couch, we slurp pizza from the box, and this mysterious "table" is clearly a waste of time, space, and lumber.

But consider. **THIS "TABLE" WILL HELP LEGITIMIZE YOUR CAVE.** It will allow guests—including family, neighbors, and kids—to eat meals without spilling burritos in their laps. Think strategy. Short term: less independence. Long term: greater acceptance of your cave.

You must lose some battles to win the war.

TEPHEN ROSE

WANTED IT TO LOOK LIKE SOMETHING A TEENAGER
OM THE 70s WOULD HAVE ACTUALLY PUT TOGETHER from stuff
ically found in mom and dad's basement. I didn't want it to look too go
trived, or like a 70s living room. *How it started:* I'm a child of the 70s
s trying to hunt down some vintage stereo equipment, and I thought

this stuff needs to be in a 70s environment. ▪ 60s–70s vintage ashtrays. They're all authentic. Not reproductions. ▪ CABLE REEL TABLE: IT'S A 70S ICON. ▪ Only 60s–70s music is allowed in the 70s man cave. ▪ The 8-track player (Pioneer HR-99) came

from a good friend, gratis, when he found out I was looking for a vintage 8-track. *Favorite things to do:* Have friends over, play cards, listen to 70s rock—and watch an occasional 70s movie classic. 〞

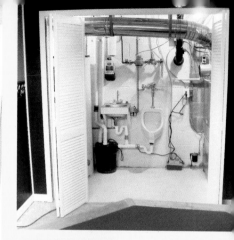

Look at these bathrooms. They're stunning. Clean, decorative, manly. **NEVER LET IT BE SAID THAT MEN ARE SLOBS.**

At every turn, cynics will tell you that "man cave" sounds juvenile, ugly, and gross. If you've installed a bathroom, here's an excellent response that will correct such misconceptions: "The man cave is a great place to take a dump."

The Collector's Cave

2

Think of yourself as a museum curator. Like a museum, you collect valuable pieces of art, you suggest a donation from your guests (usually in the form of a six-pack), you treat your collection with respect, and you stop at nothing to improve and to grow. Unlike a museum curator, you've never been stuffed in a locker.

Wade Miller

Do you prefer Coke or Pepsi?

My wife and I have been married fourteen years. At our rehearsal dinner, she and I exchanged gifts. She gave me a little shelf that had a Coke sign on it. After that, I started picking up things with Coke written on them. Flea markets, auctions. Lots of the fun of collecting is in the search for items. People would come over, see it, and usually have something they wanted to give me.

How about the building itself?

Originally built by my grandfather. It was a camp house for my uncle when he was a little boy.

❝When you walk into my backyard, you think that you have walked back in time and came up on an old country store. Gas pump and all.❞

Where'd you get the vision to convert it?

I saw the picture of an old store, and got the idea that it would be neat to make it look like an old country store. I had this idea for several years before I could afford to start building on it.

How much work did it take?

The inside was just 2x4 framing. I spent a week of vacation covering the outside and replacing the shingle roof with tin. I made the front porch out of brick pavers, and the old rusty tin came from the top of my grandfather's old barn.

And the inside?

I once saw a tin shed built over a bar in a steakhouse. I loved the look, so while I was building my bar, I incorporated it into my theme. I left the rafters exposed to hang things from. I just love the old junk hanging down from them.

Where else do you find this stuff?

I love "plundering" around old houses in the winter. (Too many snakes and wasps in the summer.) I've found many old soda bottles this way. Some are pretty rare. I found a Louisiana Big Chief bottle under an old house one day and crawled under to get it. When I crawled out from under the house, I felt something watching me. I turned. A coachwhip snake and I were looking eye to eye.

"They belonged to my grandfather. Granddad I called him. He and I were really close and I thought he walked on water. After he died I was given a pair of his boots. I hung them together and it's one of the first things that you see when you walk in the door."

PSYCHOLOGICAL ROOTS OF THE MAN CAVE

Okay. Serious time. What makes us do this? Why do we build man caves? We saved you a $400-an-hour session and talked with psychiatrist Dr. Scott Haltzman, the founder and editor of 365Reasons.com and DrScott.com, and the author of *The Secrets of Happily Married Men*, *The Secrets of Happily Married Women*, and *The Secrets of Happy Families*. That's a lot of secrets.

PSYCHOLOGICALLY, WHY DO GUYS BUILD MAN CAVES?

From studies of male psychology, we know that men tend to get overwhelmed with excessive stimuli. They tend to get overly stressed when things feel out of their control. In their domestic life, that might mean their wife making requests. It might mean getting bills that they're not able to pay. At work, it might be getting deluged with email.

SO THE CAVE HELPS CREATE ORDER?

Or block out the things that are disordering them. There's a "man cave" in his own head, too. There's a space that a man is in, even if he can't decorate it. When he's staring at a wall, he could be *emotionally* in that space. And perhaps a man cave, ultimately, ends up being a manifestation of what goes on in a man's brain.

HUH. KINDA SCARY.

In *Men Are from Mars, Women Are from Venus*, John Gray talked about a man going into his cave. That might have morphed in our vernacular. Women would say to men, "You're just going into your cave," and it's just a small step from *metaphorically* going into your cave to *literally* going into your cave.

IS THIS HEALTHY OR UNHEALTHY?

Absolutely a healthy thing. It's like anything else: it has to be in moderation. But men can sometimes build up a resentment. From my own experience, all the posters I owned from college have disappeared over the years. They're up in the attic, or they've been sold in garage sales. The great loss was when my wife sold my jean jacket—

NOT THE JEAN JACKET!

At a certain point, a man can feel like he's lost control of his home and has no sense of identity or relationship with it, particularly in the places he likes to relax, like in the TV room or his bedroom.

SO THIS HELPS HIM TAKE BACK CONTROL?

It's not an issue of "taking control back," it's an issue of minimizing resentment. If I can say to myself, "I have this space," I can emotionally overlook all the other areas in my life in which I *don't* have space.

WHAT WOULD YOUR MAN CAVE LOOK LIKE?

A lot of leather. [Pauses.] I should say a lot of leather *furniture*. When a psychiatrist says he likes leather, right away people have thoughts about his predilections. [Laughs.] It would obviously have a flatscreen TV and a surround sound system. Every man cave has to have that.

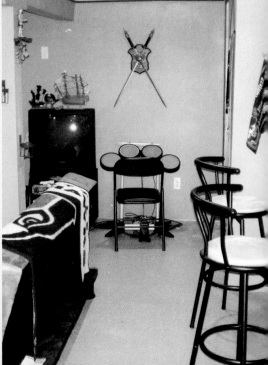

IF YOU HAVE A WEAPON, HANG IT. Guns, knives, swords, scimitars—it's impossible to have too many. This is an excellent system for defense and deterrent, much like our nuclear arsenal. It keeps rogue states (i.e., neighbors) in check, it's within easy reach, and it gives the kids something safe to play with.

ROBERT BUTTERFIELD

"When Dale Earnhardt was killed on the last lap of the Daytona 500 in 2001, I went on a collection frenzy and bought every die cast I could find. ▪ ALL THE COLLECTOR CLOCKS ARE SET AT 3:00 TO COMMEMORATE DALE. ▪ I'm transferring approximately two hundred VCR tape recordings of NASCAR races from the mid 80s through 2001, complete with commercials, which really take you back. ▪ It takes just shy of five hours to clean the room. Dusting everything would seem like a nightmare but it's fun for me, another excuse to play with my toys. ▪ A quarter-scale

Dale Earnhardt Inc. NASCAR engine that's autographed by Dale Earnhardt Jr., his stepmother Teresa Earnhardt, Steve Park, Michael Waltrip, and the president of Action Collectibles. ▪ It really irritates me that some look at man caves as being owned by redneck male chauvinists. Rooms like this are a way to express one's passion and interests—sometimes on a grand scale—and shouldn't be gender-biased. BUT MAKE NO MISTAKE, IF YOU SHOW UP TO MY CAVE WEARING A PASTEL SWEATER TIED AROUND YOUR NECK, WHITE PANTS, AND SPORTING THE CLASSIC HARVARD ACCENT AND CORPORATE LAUGH, ASKING HOW MY STOCK PORTFOLIO IS DOING, I WILL SWIFTLY KNOCK YOU ON YOUR ASS and toss you out to the curb."

The Sports Cave

3

You will never play in the NFL. You will never circle the bases in Yankee Stadium. You owe it to yourself, therefore, to do the next best thing: create a shrine to your team that's so spectacular, so heroic, that it actually improves your team's chance of winning. You can't explain how this works. But you know it does.

WHY SHOULD YOU BUILD A MAN CAVE?

Maybe you're on the fence. You're thinking this is too costly, too time consuming, too corny, too hard a sell to your spouse. Fair questions. The answers:

YOU CAN BUILD WITHOUT MAN-GUILT. You get a pass. This is the one time in your life you can be an interior designer without feeling like a wimp.

IT REFLECTS YOU. This can't be stressed enough. The goal isn't to mimic a cheesy beer commercial; the goal is to create a space that reflects *your personality.* It can be a library, a casino, a shrine to foreign cinema.

IT HONORS YOUR PAST. Think about your guilty pleasures. The golden reminders of high school, college, or your time in juvenile delinquency. Chances are, the relics of these eras are stuffed in boxes, ignored, hidden. Reclaim them.

LADIES LOVE THEM. Still single? A man cave is a chick magnet. There's nothing women find sexier than sheet-covered sofas, Corona statues, and empty pizza boxes.

IT'S A REPRIEVE FROM REALITY. As in, once you're in your cave long enough, you might think the above is true.

IT'S A BUDDY HANGOUT. This is almost reason enough. Once you have your space, you will suddenly have a venue where all your friends congregate. Don't have friends? With a good enough cave, you will.

IT'S A SAFE, QUIET, HAPPY PLACE. Every shrink talks about going to your "safe, quiet, and happy place." Enough metaphors. Instead of daydreaming, why not just build it?

IT'S AN ENDURING PROJECT. This is a hobby that you will return to again and again, tweaking, improving, constantly adding new elements. A man cave is forever, like diamonds and herpes.

ALFRED WASILEWSKI

"IT STARTED WITH THE CARPETING, which needed to be replaced after a flood. Then I had to paint the walls to match. After that, I was inspired to add memorabilia. The final part was convincing my wife to swap out the tan furniture with Giants-themed furniture. ▪ THE INSPIRATION WAS THE GIANTS' IMPROBABLE WIN OF SUPER BOWL XLII AGAINST THE PATRIOTS. I started with that Giants team, but then quickly realized that I had to honor the Giants of yesteryear. ▪ Every man, especially a married man, should have

his own space, or man cave. A place of refuge. A place to let your inner manliness come out without risk of criticism, nagging, or judgment. ▪ WOMEN HAVE THEIR BATHROOMS WITH SCENTED CANDLES, BATH GELS AND OILS, AND WHALE MUSIC; MEN NEED THEIR PLACE OF TRANQUILLITY. ▪ I started with putting up framed photos of Giants players. Slowly, over time, I was able to replace every photo with a duplicate that was signed by the player. ▪ I found Giants-themed projection slides, and I set the system up in the cave to shine on the ceiling. ▪ I was creating a framed collage for Super Bowl XXI, but I couldn't find a suitable picture of Phil Simms in action. I eventually called the Giants head office, and they put me in touch with the Giants official photographer, who found one in his archives and sent it to me. ▪ (Thank you, Mark Fordham, for taking these great pictures of my cave.)❞

Aesthetic principle of man caves: **ANY BLANK WALL CAN BE IMPROVED** with a colorful, life-size poster of a man you have never met.

GREG (BUBBA) RASER

"This is a 'blue-collar' man cave, for guys with dirty hands. No fancy mirrors, wine glasses, imported wood paneling, or trim. Look at it. It's all particleboard. ▪ THE MAN CAVE WAS AN 'AWG' DESIGN: AS WE GO. ▪ This is no Barrett-Jackson auction house, not a lot of bling . . . just small town hospitality.

▪ It took me thirty-five years to get a nice shop and man cave. I did a lot of car, farm tractor, and truck repairs in the ol' garage, with no insulation, and a kerosene torpedo heater—yuck. Now I can bring something out in the man cave, and work on it without noise blasting from the heater, or fumes burning my eyes. ▪ There are some real pretty man caves out there, full of Corvettes and hot rods, but I really like mine."

You're a man of action. So you don't simply watch games in your man cave—you play them, you win them. And **POKER NIGHT IS THE PERFECT MAN CAVE ACTIVITY**. It works. It's more social than a football game. It's more interactive than a movie. It's more focused than a random night of drinking.

THE WIRED CAVE

Some caves are simple. And some have gadgets, lots of gadgets. For the latter, we grill *Wired*'s Daniel Dumas, product reviewer and associate editor.

LET'S SAY I'M STARTING A CAVE FROM SCRATCH. I'M READY FOR GADGETS. WHERE SHOULD I START?
The TV is the key to the whole setup. Go as large as the room will hold: 1080p resolution. Make sure it has Internet connectivity. Netflix streaming.

WHAT ABOUT 3D?
I'm skeptical. I don't see it trickling out of the theater and into your man cave. Think about the glasses. They cost $80. Let's say you invite ten friends for the Super Bowl. That's $800. On top of that, are you going to turn to your friend after a touchdown, and high-five him with those stupid-ass glasses on? [Laughs.] Right now the technology is in its infancy: 3D could be like Betamax or HD DVD.

IF YOU'RE FILTHY-UGLY-I-HATE-YOU RICH, WHAT'S THE BEST WAY TO SPEND YOUR DOUGH?
Audio. You can go balls-to-the-walls crazy. There are companies that will come in to your room, measure your acoustics, judge the materials of your walls, and they'll make a custom audio system. This is the kind of thing NBA players do. You can spend $100,000.

AND TO SAVE CASH?
Especially if your man cave is on the smaller side, you can get a wireless speaker box. It looks like a long, petrified dinosaur turd—

—PERFECT FOR A MAN CAVE—
—and it creates the illusion that the sound is happening all around you, but it's coming from one place. You can get one for around $200. And it's a hell of a lot better than the speakers that are integrated into the TV. It's what I have in my apartment.

WHAT DO YOU SEE FOR THE FUTURE OF GADGETS IN MAN CAVES, IN 2020, SAY?
I assume it will be some sort of robot that will provide some sort of sexual gratification. [Laughs.]

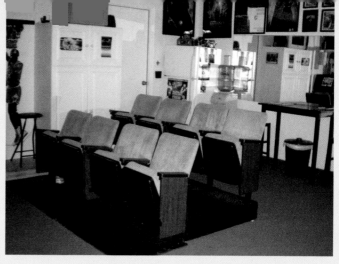

WHEN IN DOUBT, MAKE IT BIGGER.

Its secondary purpose is to show movies, its primary purpose is to show off sound systems that, if used properly, will damage both your hearing and your brain.

MARK STURTEVANT

"Since I built this room, I've gotten back to the roots of music-listening. It seems everyone is on the go, with the convenience of MP3 players, streaming music, and smart phones. I had gotten away from the days of just focusing on the music itself. Now, I make the time to just relax and enjoy the artists, the way the music was meant to be enjoyed. It's the center of the *experience*, not just a soundtrack for a hectic life. ▪ WE NOW SPEND MORE TIME IN THE CAVE THAN MOST OF THE REST OF THE HOUSE. ▪ I bought my guitar and amp fourteen years or so ago, when I was in a small garage band playing for fun. ▪ This fridge

was made in the 50s. It's still going as strong as ever; it's outlasted at least four others we bought. MY FIANCÉE HAS TRIED TO GET ME TO SELL IT OVER THE YEARS, AND I TOLD HER THAT YOU WOULD HAVE TO PRY IT OUT OF MY COLD, DEAD HANDS."

Still think man caves are only for meatheads? Then you don't know bands. Most musicians are pack rats, gear hoarders, lovers of equipment— old and new. This stuff accumulates.

With a music-themed man cave, you create your own mini studio. **INSTEAD OF USING YOUR AMP AS A NIGHTSTAND, YOU CAN MAKE IT AN ALTAR.**

If you go this route, one tip: soundproof.

HALLMARKS OF A GOOD CAVE

There's only one true success criterion: your own satisfaction. That's what counts. If you think it works, it works. That said, certain elements distinguish a just-okay-for-the-owner man cave from a spectacular man cave.

THEMATIC COHERENCE The best caves are *about* something. At a glance, you get it. The theme can be anything: the Texas Longhorns, the Peloponnesian War, My Little Pony. (If you choose My Little Pony, no sweat, just do one thing for us: please immediately jump off the tallest building you can find.)

CLEANLINESS Yep. You read that right. Keep it clean, or, at least, keep it odor-free. There's nothing manly or cool about fungus.

COMFORT You know those *gorgeous* sofas? Sleek, modern, but not very comfortable? They're not welcome here.

THAT "ONE AWESOME THING" There should be something that sets your cave apart. Flip through this book and you'll see all kinds of wacky, singular features.

USABILITY Don't take your eye off the ball. Remember, you go in your cave to actually *do* something. Make sure you have multiple options for entertainment, whether that's TV, music, pool, darts, poker, or an indoor rock-climbing wall (see page 164).

Mike Petinarelis

How'd this get started?

It wasn't supposed to be a man cave. It was just supposed to be an extra washroom. We knew we wanted a sauna, and my wife really wanted a bidet. [Laughs.]

A bidet, really?

You know, the thing that sprays your ass with water? So I'm thinking, do you really want to *use that*? Thank God, one of her girlfriends talked her out of it, and said, "Look, if it's that bad back there, just hop in the shower."

And then . . .

But I'd already put in the drain for this thing, so I'm thinking, what am I going to *put* there? I thought, you know what, I'm going to put a urinal in here. And my wife ends up getting

Eco-friendly waterless urinal ❝It doesn't have a water-flusher. In the top pee-trap, there's a chemical that you pour in, and your pee doesn't stink. So you just flush it out once a month with a bucket of water, and you're good.❞

❝You can't find a Kleenex box that is masculine. They all have plastic colors, they're all pastel. So I found this Kleenex website, and had the box custom made.❞

pregnant, so she can't use the sauna because of the heat, and then it's just me down there. Then I thought, okay, this will be my man cave. It just snowballed.

You have a truly stylish space.

I'm interested in architecture; I read a lot of men's magazines. And this just fits my personality. It's clean. It's simple. A lot of strong, square, geometric, masculine colors.

Most man caves are places where all the buddies hang out. Is that the case with your sauna?

[Laughs.] No. It's basically just for me. If another guy wants to hop in the sauna with me, I'll probably tell him, "I'll wait outside, but by all means go inside and do your thing."

How much time do you spend in there?

Probably six to seven hours a week.

Whattaya do in there?

Mostly reading. I've got a stereo system, two speakers in the washroom and two in the sauna. And I've got a little gaming system, so I sort of sit on the toilet and play my video games.

Every man's dream.

"I would have some of my soldiers over, and the man cave was a place to hang out. I could keep an eye on my soldiers and keep them out of trouble. It was a sanctuary—a place to go on retreat, to talk about the military, and to teach and train my soldiers on how to be great and better soldiers." —*Cave owner Marty Peterson*

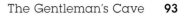

Joe Bottieri

How'd this start?

Back in October 2008, I came across a cabinet shop that was closing its doors for good due to the housing decline. I had no intention of building a man cave, but I wanted a larger garage and workshop where I could work on stuff (in other words, hide). I made a cash offer.

Tell us about the space's conversion.

First, the place had to be cleaned. Then the walls had to be scraped, as there was splattered glue all over them, and hardware had to be removed.

Damn. Sounds like a lot of work.

I rented a commercial concrete floor grinder and spent ten days grinding the floor smooth. I removed all the glue that wouldn't come off with a scraper.

Pretty sweet ceilings and walls.

They were covered with compressed air lines—some of which I removed—and I installed new electrical conduit to bring the place up to code. The ceiling had to be insulated, so five and a half inches of sprayed-in foam did a nice job.

I like the stage.

I built the stage and bar by hand, myself. Under both the stage and bar area, I put down a vapor barrier of vinyl

flooring before building them in place. I also used pressure-treated wood where it contacted the exterior concrete block walls.

Do you have experience with that type of work?

Never worked with wood or built anything like that before.

Wow. Nice work. What do you like to do in there?

Live music! I have many friends who are professional musicians. They come to the cave to practice with their band. Whenever there's a combo, we call a party for friends to come enjoy the live music. The cave depicts the three material loves of my lifetime: motorcycles, cars, and music.

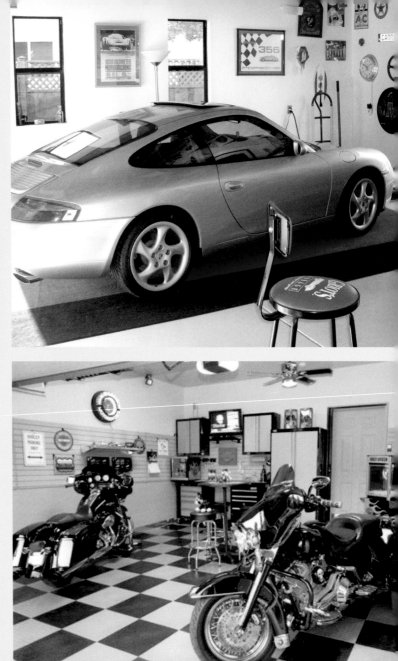

In something of a paradox, you can turn your garage into a man cave that turns into . . . a garage. **YOU WILL ONLY UNDERSTAND THIS IF YOU HAVE THE RIGHT WHEELS**.

WARREN CALVERT

❝THE MAN CAVE ROOM IS ACTUALLY OLDER THAN THE HOUSE ITSELF, which was built by a Union Civil War sergeant in 1866. ▪ The bar is an old railroad depot counter that came from Nebraska. It's more than a hundred years old. ▪ THIS MAN CAVE CERTAINLY HAS A MYSTERY BEHIND IT. When I pulled a worktable away from a wall, I found a couple of shackle rings attached to the bricks. I was a little puzzled, as the house was built *after* the Civil War ended, and the original owner fought on the Union side. But I researched further, and the house sits on two lots, and one part belonged to William T. Wood, who was elected president at the Missouri Slaveholders Convention. ▪ The framed Olajuwan jersey was a gift from 7-Up for ordering a large quantity of two-liters when I worked at a drug store.**❞**

We have to admit it. We kind of want these
shadow-women in every room in our house.

You have to admire the bold simplicity.
No innuendo, no subtlety, no cheeky
references: just . . . breasts.

Cave Law: never
serve your mother
with this glass.

We're not sure exactly
what this is used for. And
we don't ever want to know.

Is this supposed to look like what we
think it looks like?

A great room for the whole family to enjoy.

The Bar Cave

The bar is the new fireplace. It's the lifeblood of your cave. It gives purpose and it gives joy. And it's the only establishment that lets you wear pajamas.

THE WISE MAN WILL INSTALL A BAR COMPLETE WITH STOOLS, COASTERS, VARNISH, AND A BOWL OF CASHEWS.
The fact that sitting at a stool is bad for your back, sort of weird to do at home, and is never–*never!*–as comfortable as flopping on a couch? Irrelevant.

If you cared *only* about comfort, you would simply furnish the room with a mattress, lying down so you could stare at your ceiling-mounted TV. But you're a man of society. You're a gentleman. The bar provides a gathering spot for other such gentlemen, letting you discuss important topics like the midterm elections, the novels of Murakami, and who can belch the loudest.

As you can see from this slew of photos, there are endless shapes, sizes, and ways to give yourself alcohol poisoning.

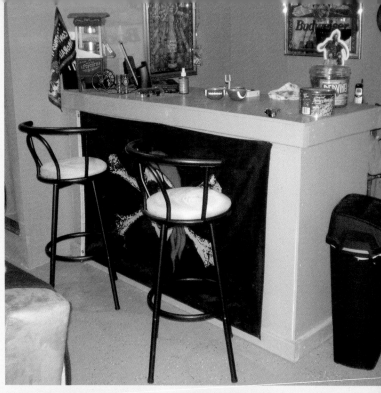

ALL THAT'S MISSING IS YOU!

MAN CAVE ON A BUDGET

USE EBAY AND CRAIGSLIST. Only the thinnest of lines separates worthless from priceless. At any given moment, thousands of coasters, gumball machines, and dartboards are sold online and sold on the cheap. One man's trash is another man's treasure.

RECYCLE. You already have most of what you need for your cave. They're frozen in deep storage, trapped, stuck in attics and closets and basements. These are the hideously glorious decorations of your past, the items deemed "too juvenile" to get plum placement in the living room. Rescue these gems.

BUILD SLOWLY. Don't build it overnight. Start small, start simple, and only add features as time and money permits. To begin, you just need the Essentials (see page 14). Think of your cave like a relationship—one that you will nurture over time, one that will grow, and one that never ends in tears or court.

USE YOUR FRIENDS. Once you build your cave, over time, your friends will start bringing you decorative gifts. You don't have to ask, they'll just do it. (See page 133 for the Snowball Effect.) This has less to do with generosity, really, than with the fact that your house is more convenient than the dump.

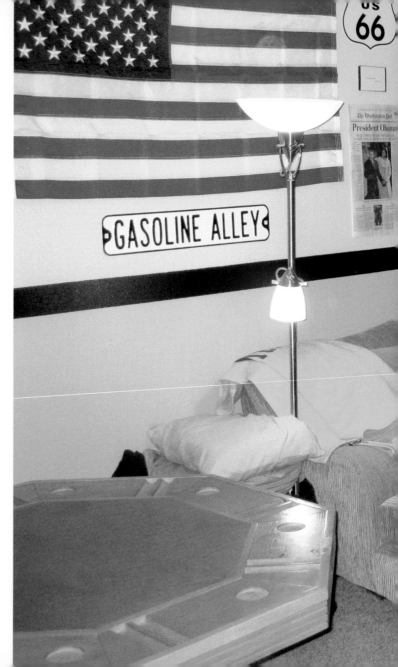

The space program has stalled. A cure for cancer does not seem imminent. The only truly great invention of the last twenty years was the DVR. But do not despair! The great spirit of **AMERICAN INNOVATION IS NOT DEAD. IT LIVES. AND IT LIVES IN THE MAN CAVE.** The greatest minds in the field have found new, exciting, radical ways to guzzle booze faster.

Andrew Crout-Hamel

The tiki bar. How was this born?

I was in the Navy Seals. I had a ton of pictures from when I was on the parachuting team. The pictures had been in boxes for years, and I started hanging them up on the garage walls. Around then, my wife and I went to an outdoor extravaganza expo, and I saw a tiki bar for sale. I thought, *man*, I've gotta have that . . .

You gotta *have that.*

And that same day I bought a pool table at the expo—they were clearing everything out. Once I had the tiki bar, it just started to grow. People started bringing me things. People would drop things off and say, "Hey! This would be great for the tiki bar!"

What'd they bring?

> For my birthday, one guy brought me a Jimmy Buffett margarita machine. Another guy brought me a Jägermeister machine. A popcorn maker. It just started to grow.

I see a bit of a "rum theme" here . . .

> I bought an oak barrel, and it's full of Captain Morgan rum. I had an engraver engrave a Captain Morgan symbol on it. In fact, one of my dogs is named Captain Morgan.

Favorite parachuting photos?

> I retired from the Seals after twenty years, so the photos are from all over the United States. I jumped into the St. Louis Arch. I jumped into Nolan Ryan's induction into the Hall of Fame. I jumped with President George H. W. Bush for his seventy-fifth birthday. I jumped with the wrestling announcer who says, "Let's get ready to rumble!" I've got more than 7,200 jumps.

Advice to other guys building their cave?

> Don't try and build it so quickly. Everybody has some favorite things that have been in a box or a closet that you couldn't hang up. You know, the rabbit with the horn on its head. Those are the things that end up in the man cave. Let it slowly develop. And eventually it will have a theme of its own.

The iconic symbol of bachelorhood. The pool table oozes class, sophistication, and leisure. **IT'S THE TOY OF A GENTLEMAN.** Especially when surrounded by antlers, hacksaws, and life-sized posters of football players.

CELEBRITY MAN CAVES

If you are reading this book, there's a good chance you're a celebrity. More and more A-listers have embraced the trend. It makes sense. Not only do man caves provide comfort, style, and peace of mind (see: every page in this book), they also provide something even more elusive: privacy. The man cave is not for paparazzi.

Just a few of the notables with man caves:

LAURENCE FISHBURNE "I have a man cave somewhere in California—a totally undisclosed location where manly things occur. There are motorcycles, there are secret doors and passageways. Women are welcome but they must knock."

BRAD PITT He doesn't have a man cave. He has man caves, plural. Pitt's pits—in New Orleans and Malibu, California—cost over $200,000 and include flatscreens, a Wurlitzer jukebox, a Harley, a Confederate Hellcat, and, because he's a man of the people, a keg-o-rator. Regular guests include Matt Damon.

NICOLAS CAGE This is a man who named his son Kal-El, so it shouldn't be a surprise that Cage's "man sanctuary" features rare Superman comics.

BILL SIMMONS Unwritten rule of sports journalism: when you write your 20,000th column on the Patriots or Celtics, you get to build your dream man cave. (On his public Facebook page, as his office, Simmons simply lists: "Man Cave.")

JOHNNY DEPP When Johnny Depp invites you to his man cave in Paris, be sure to compliment him on the guitars he keeps inside, along with the cases of wine—from his own vineyard, naturally.

GEORGE CLOONEY Yes and no. Clooney has avoided the use of the phrase "man cave," saying that he lives in "man castles." If it walks like a duck and talks like a duck . . .

BARACK OBAMA When the president redecorated the Oval Office, columnist Maureen Dowd called it a "redecorated man cave . . . with browns and beiges and leather, and it resembles an upscale hotel conference room or a 70s conversation pit."

JIM SCHORN

"Back in 1986 I started working in the auto industry as a mechanic. We had 'tool guys' visit the shop once a week. I'd go out to their trucks to buy tools, and I noticed they also sold these die cast semis. I started buying them.

■ Seems everywhere I would go, they were selling shot glasses, so I'd buy one

or two or three. I have some from Germany, Norway, the Dominican Republic, Hong Kong, Mexico, Paris, and Canada. ■ I HAVE A NICE EUROPEAN BEER GLASS COLLECTION. A Vegas collection, a Renaissance Festival goblet collection, a pint glass collection, some old Minnesota Vikings glasses, and I also have one shelf of glasses that I got from my grandma."

Collections and Approximate Quantities

Beer lights 15
Die cast trucks 150
Lighted clocks 8
Beer cans displayed 150
Beer cans in boxes 200
Gatornational 70
Beer trays 25
Can/bottle openers 45

Very few things in life are as useless, inoperable, or self-defeating as owning your own slot machine. Others that come close: owning your own gas pump (with no gasoline), elevator shaft (in a single-floor building), and baby crib (when you have no kids).

That said, **THEY HAVE A CERTAIN CHARM**. You can look at them and say, "No matter what, I'm a *winner*." On a rainy, gloomy day, you can cheer yourself up by thinking, "The house always wins, and I am the house."

Spaces for Man Cave

	Pros	Cons
Garage	Already feels like "man space." Wife less likely to object. Farther away from domesticity.	Concrete floor. Smells like gasoline. You no longer have a garage.
Shack	More charm than indoor space. Virile. Allows more flexibility in construction. Lets you feel like a badass.	Electricity? Plumbing? HD cable? Also . . . dude, you're living in a *shack*.
Basement	Remote. Partitioned. Private. AC-friendly. If you have it, use it.	Stairs.
Attic	Same benefits of basement.	Often smaller. Stairs. You sort of feel like Anne Frank.
Spare room inside house	All the comforts of home (AC, carpet, bathrooms).	Noise travels. Less of a "buffer" from rest of household. Resentment might grow. That room *could* be used for a guest room or study or tea room, whatever the hell that is.
Closet	Don't laugh. If your house or apartment doesn't have any room to spare, you can still carve out a little space of your own. This will be more of a place for reflection, solitude, and a renewal of spirit.	Complete loss of self-worth.

NEVER GO THIRSTY.

As Tom Waits once said, "I don't have a drinking problem, 'cept when I can't get a drink." No one with a man cave ever has that problem.

When these guys invite you to a party, you say, "Yes."

The Clutter-as-Art Cave

6

Tragically, modern design has railed against "clutter." (Come to think of it, this is not just true of *modern* design, but also classic design, ancient design, postmodern design, and every design since Eve stumbled into Adam's man cave.)

You know better. **CLUTTER MAKES SENSE.** Clutter is efficient. Clutter works. Just look at the bounty of nature and the peak of mankind's achievements: the vegetation of a jungle, the organs of the human body, the engine of a car—the naysayers would dismiss all this, too, as mere "clutter." Where others see chaos, you see order.

When you see an empty wall, you, as a visionary, know to decorate that sucker with toy trucks, jars of pickles, and 5,000 blinking Christmas lights. There's a word for that: art.

One word: understatement.

THE SNOWBALL EFFECT

The Snowball Effect. It's an important cycle, a mysterious cycle, a wondrous cycle. It's right up there with the ecosystem and the miracle of life. Once your cave reaches a critical mass of stuff—it doesn't matter what the stuff is—it will begin to snowball.

Example: let's say your cave has a theme of the Houston Rockets. You hoard priceless relics like Yao Ming bobble head dolls, banners from the 1994–95 championships, Rockets air fresheners, an authentic jock strap worn by Hakeem Olajuwon, and when you go to the bathroom, you sure as hell wipe with Rockets toilet paper.

The beast must be fed. And others will feed the beast. The collection will grow and grow and grow, even if you buy *nothing else*, ever. Every birthday, you will get Rockets paraphernalia. When out-of-towners stay for a visit, they will thank you with Rockets-flavored chewing gum.

This is a good thing. Embrace it. And pay it forward: when your friend starts his own cave, your job is to feed his addiction.

Jeff Smith

What was your inspiration?

> I got the idea from hanging out in bars. Places like TGI Fridays. I've been collecting this stuff for over forty years. It took me eleven years to put it all together.

What kind of reaction do you usually get?

> This room has been known to scare the shit out of small children as well as some adults.

How many—ah, "collectibles"—do you have in here?

> Over ten thousand items in the cave. Including seventy-five taxidermy items, a thousand hats, a fireplace, six TVs, a 200-gallon aquarium built in the wall with piranha, horns, hides, heads, fins, feathers, and fur.

That's all?

Also 1,500 chili pepper lights.

Favorite items?

The six-foot mako shark with a Barbie doll in the mouth, the seven-foot black bear, the albino raccoon, and the giant sea turtle.

Do you think every one of these items was a good, sound purchase?

I got the turtle in a San Francisco flea market for $100. It cost me $120 to ship it home. Still having a hard time justifying that one.

Good place for a scavenger hunt.

Oftentimes when I have people over I will give them a list of a hundred items or so to find. I'll say, "You have three hours to find all the items, and if you do, you get to keep the house."

Any winners?

Nobody has, and never will!

What's the most expensive item?

My newest addition, a 9' 6" grizzly bear at $3,000.

Seems reasonable.

I get a kick out of it when people come over for the first time, and they walk in, and the first word out of their mouths is "Oh . . ." Their heads snap back, looking up. The ceiling is 9' 6" high and covered with shit. Some people complain about their necks hurting when they leave.

Other favorites?

The collection of four hundred beer tap handles, 1,200 beer coasters, the seven alligator heads, the bats in glass—this freaks out *all* the women. And the wild boar's head from a 200-pound pig is pretty cool, along with the full-mounted badger, the armadillo, the eight raccoons, and rattlesnake hides.

You could get lost in there.

You can stare at a section, walk away, come back later, and see some totally different things in the same place. It's like an onion; just keep peeling away the layers.

What do you do in there?

Beer. And watching sports. And beer, and beer. The more you drink the deader the animals become. They are as dead as Julius Caesar.

DAN DIXON

"MY FIRST MAN CAVE STARTED IN 1968 WHILE I WAS ATTENDING COLLEGE ON THE GI BILL. For about thirty-two years, I worked for the forest service and moved every couple of years. I always found a small space in a toolshed or room to hide in. The book *Men Are from Mars, Women Are from Venus* was my first clue this was normal. ▪ THREE FAVORITE THINGS IN MAN CAVE: MY FATHER'S ASHES. MY GRANDFATHER'S TOOLS. MY FISHING REELS. ▪ The only real sharing

is through the doggie door, and she doesn't mess with the stuff. ▪ The cave is a retreat and sanctuary. It is where I look inward and where I put things into perspective. The only person always welcome is my bride of forty-six years who seldom comes in. It is becoming a special place for my grandkids to visit on the rare occasions they are with us. The younger ones see the magic. **"**

HOW TO CONVINCE YOUR WIFE

YOU'RE A HEARTBEAT AWAY. Let's say she's in the kitchen and has a life-threatening emergency. Say she needs you to open the jar of strawberry jam. You can be there in twenty minutes flat, barring overtime.

CAVE BEATS BAR. The logic is unshakable. [A] You have friends [B] You spend time with your friends [C] That time is often spent at a bar [D] The bar involves alcohol, driving, and money [E] The cave saves money and eliminates the risk of sloppy driving. Careful, though. The sentence, "Honey, I'm *bringing the bar to our home!*" is less compelling than you'd think.

IT'S FOR THE FAMILY, TOO. Invite the kids, invite the women—occasionally. Why would she assume that the cave is only for a *man*? What could give her that impression?

YOU WILL NOT HIDE. She's worried this will be your bunker. That you will submerge in the cave, buy a cot, use a bedpan, and only come up once a week to replenish supplies. Not true. Who needs a bedpan? You will install plumbing. More seriously—give her some realistic time parameters. This is crucial.

IT CORDONS OFF THE FILTH. Many cities zone off certain districts—the slums in the east, the churches in the west. With the cave, like a sensible mayor, you institute zoning. The rest of the home is now free of bums (your friends), hard drugs (beer cans), prostitution (pin-up girls), and crime (your relaxation).

GREG BATTLESON

BUILDER AWARD

"THIS EVOLVED FROM THE SUBTERRANEAN
DECAYING BRICK FOUNDATION of a six-family apartment
building in the city. It originally was a soot-covered dingy basement . . . with
a coal-converted furnace in the boiler room, gas meters and electric meters
beneath a stairwell, and old "coal storage" bins that stretched
the length of the building. ▪ THE ORIGINAL IDEA WAS NOT
TO BUILD A MAN CAVE AT ALL . . . when all the cleanup and
painting was done, I simply wanted to set up a workshop
in the boiler room for maintenance of the apartments
and storage of my tools and house supplies. I eventually

started spending so much time down here with building things and fix-up projects, that I decided to frame out an office in one of the little alcoves in the basement. A makeshift desk, some old bookcases, a TV and a computer made the place almost livable, so I decided to put a bed down here—one of the storage bins became a bedroom. THEN ALL MY HOBBIES, INTERESTS, AND COLLECTIONS STARTED OVERRUNNING THE PLACE. THAT WAS FIFTEEN YEARS AGO!"

"Any room has six sides to it, so I made sure to engineer the room to address the ceiling and the floor, not just the walls. Items are hung on the ceiling to keep your eyes moving around the room, and the floor has a checkered pattern to look like a victory lane. With items sticking out from the ceiling and walls, it gives you that 3D kind of feel. **IT'S A ROOM THAT LITERALLY BITCH-SLAPS EACH ONE OF YOUR FIVE SENSES.**" *–Robert Butterfield*

Odd & Outdoor Caves

7

The cave that's not a cave. Without a doubt, these are some of the coolest types of spaces. They live in a backyard or a forest or a patch of land in Australia. They're mysterious. They're disguised.

From a casual glance, they look like shacks or huts. Maybe they hold wheelbarrows and lawnmowers. They're probably deserted. And can we be honest? They even look a little ... creepy ... like the perfect setting for *Saw XIV*.

Then ... you open the door. And you're teleported into a magical world of manliness. Behold.

John Bryant

Dude. You have a man castle. What gave you the idea?

My gardening-fanatic wife forced me to take her on a garden crawl of Europe. I hated the gardens, but fell in love with the sixteenth- and seventeenth-century architecture. Old abbeys, cathedrals, follies, and towers.

Who built it?

I designed the tower, then built it myself with my own hands, no help.

Sounds easy.

My first challenge was to get the county to approve my plans to build the tower. The officer looked at my plans and said, "Mate, I've been in this job thirty-five years, and I ain't never seen one of these suckers." It then took nearly one year of arguing and debating to get final approval.

You must be a construction guy by trade, right?

I'm a white-collar guy. I'd never built anything before. The tower was my effort at doing something with my hands. I laid block in winter freeze and summer heat. It took me two and a half years, but I did it.

Since you're a construction rookie, did you have any close calls?

A very sharp Stanley knife was sitting on top of a ladder, and it fell off and hit me on the top of my head. Luckily it hit me blunt end first; if it had been the sharp end, you would not be reading this. After that I went and bought a hard hat.

What's the reaction from women?

Every woman who sees it says, "Why on earth would anyone build *that*?" And they couldn't care less, except when I tell them that women are not permitted, and then they go nuts wanting to see inside.

Favorite things inside your cave?

Mummified dead cat. Mummified dead rat. A fiberglass "son of a bitch," which is a life-sized dog designed to hang over the tailgate of a pickup truck. A life-sized Chinese terracotta warrior.

What do people, um . . . do up there?

My tower has become a place of prayer, meditation, and contemplation. I now have a number of Christian friends who "book in" to enjoy the solitude and serenity. One guy stayed three days, praying and fasting.

You can find more about John Bryant's cave at www.towerbloke.com.

ROBBY BRYANT

" I was always into military aviation. I served in the Air Force during Desert Shield and Desert Storm. I mean, what kid doesn't want to grow up and be a fighter pilot? That's how I got the idea for my room. ▪ I WANTED TO GIVE IT A SQUADRON-READY ROOM FEEL. ▪ I never had the opportunity to actually fly jets, but man, I would have loved to. ▪ Flight gear is the physical, tangible piece of aviation history that speaks to the courage and sacrifice of the pilots—from all generations and all wars. What better way to honor

the sacrifice and the people? ▪ They came from the US government, eBay, and some private collectors. They run the gamut from HGU-2s, to HGU-33s, HGU-55s, and HGU-68s. ▪ Government gear is sold in lots, and one shipment had some chemical warfare suits and hoods in it, too. My brother picked up the shipment in his truck, and he got stopped for a busted taillight. The local police open the boxes and there's all of these chemical warfare suits, gas mask hoods, etc. The police officer thought he had uncovered some sort of homegrown terrorist plot, and the next thing I know, I have the FBI coming to pay me a little visit about my purchase. That's your tax dollars at work for you! ▪ A Marine friend of mine sent me A LITTLE GLASS BOTTLE FILLED WITH BLACK SAND FROM THE BEACH ON IWO JIMA. THIS IS THE THING I HOLD DEAREST, because of the blood spilled on

that sand and the human sacrifices made on it. ▪ You really get a sense of what military aviation is all about by looking around the cave when you're in it. You see the sweat stains, and the faded flight suits, and just wonder what these things would say if they could speak. „

DOES A SINGLE GUY NEED A MAN CAVE?

Hey, Single Guy. Listen up. We know what you're thinking: *I'm single. I can do whatever I want, whenever I want, wherever I want. I answer to no wife.*

This is misguided and shortsighted. Sure, maybe you don't *need* a man cave. But you *should* have one. It will improve the quality of your life, subtly, like adding vegetables to your diet. You can design, create, and improve a space that matches your own vision, whatever that vision might be.

All men, even single ones, still need the illusion of propriety, of respectability. The bulk of your living-space still needs to look *normal*. When you bring a girl home, she'll freak out if she sees your entire apartment converted into a replica of the Death Star. You need a place for this, a hidden lair tucked away.

ERIC (GAZOO) FACCIO

"My wife and I differ on decorating themes. She likes 'contemporary' and I like 'wilderness and stuffed critters.' ▪ My wife and I make about fifty-four gallons of wine a season. That's about 270 bottles a year for the cave. Wife and friends of wife always like wine, so why not? TWO GLASSES OF ANYTHING WE MAKE AND THEY'RE WELL-LUBRICATED, PLIABLE LIKE BUTTER. ▪ Nothing better than the one you love with a little Love Potion #9 in 'em. . . . Remember, beer goggles work for chicks too. . . . Heck, I've been married for over twenty years. . . . Gotta be doing something right? Maybe it's the Potion? ▪ *Favorite thing to do in the cave:* Have Sex! And lots of it! Oh yeah, baby. . . . I even have a cavern for it. ▪ Ninety-five percent of all trophies were harvested or caught by myself. All were cleaned and then consumed by

the cave inhabitants. ▪ MY CAVE STARTED WITH FOUR CEMENT WALLS, TWO SUMP-PUMP HOLES, AND THAT'S IT. I didn't want to burden my family and friends with helping on my adventure, so I did everything myself. ▪ My cave is over two thousand square feet. It has three main caves and six caverns."

BUILDER AWARD

THE WOMAN CAVE?

*F*irst of all, it's called a Lady Lair," *says Rachel Hardage, a women's magazine editor who has worked at Glamour, Real Simple, and most recently Southern Living. She gives us a behind-the-scenes tour.*

Come on in. The door's unlocked, but I can't open it because my nails are wet. May I offer you some Tasti D-Lite? We have light (vanilla) and dark (chocolate) on tap. Oh, don't be shy—make yourself comfortable on the couch. It's from Anthropologie. Yeah, we know. Lotsa pillows. We got them on Etsy, and we like to throw them at each other when we have pillow fights in our underwear.

What would you like to watch? Here in the Lady Lair we pretty much stick to the Molly Ringwald/Meg Ryan genre, with the occasional Lifetime movie starring Tori Spelling, so take your pick from our color-coded DVD collection. Look in the magenta section. Ma-gen-ta. (Sigh.) Okay, see that

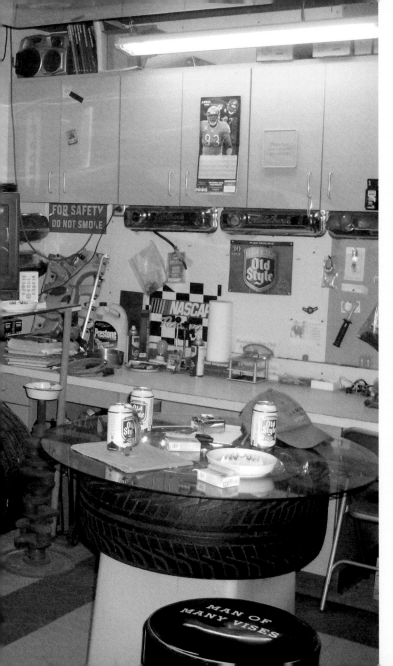

purplish-pink? Yeah, that's it. Okay, before we watch, we like to adjust our television settings so that female celebrities look as wide as possible. Yeah, that's better! Tori Swelling!

Okay, now we'll dim this pink chandelier from ABC Carpet & Home and light a few scented candles that smell like all the foods we don't allow ourselves to eat. What's that heavenly smell, you ask? I think that candle's called "Cinnabon" (it's Bridget's favorite!), but I prefer this "Popeye's Chicken" pillar over here....

Movie's over! Tori slept with Danger, despite her mother's warning, and now we're going to play some darts! Yes, Lady Lairs have darts. Sort of. We throw our sharpest stiletto heels at photos of our ex-boyfriends while listening to Taylor Swift. Five points for an eye, three points for a ... oh, wait—isn't that your face up on the wall? I'm very sorry, but I believe it's time to exit the Lady Lair. No, you can't take your Tasti D-Lite.

—Rachel Hardage

IF YOU KILLED IT, MOUNT IT. UNLESS IT
ONLY HAS TWO LEGS, IN WHICH CASE,
BURY IT.

CARY OF SACRAMENTO

66 We found a new home with a large bonus room over the garage. I spent months designing and planning. My key requirements included: 1) a complete home office; 2) two Xbox setups for group gaming; 3) a full home theater setup with four leather recliners and a vented AV cabinet I could access from the back; 4) AS MUCH INDOOR ROCK WALL–CLIMBING SPACE AS I COULD SQUEEZE OUT OF IT. ▪ *Buttkickers:* These are physical subwoofers that attach to the chairs. They cause the chairs to rumble when there are explosions, gunfire, and lion growls. ▪ There are fifteen layers of carpet pad on the floor in all the climbing wall area. Kids (and grown-ups) can fall wherever, and the floor will take the impact. ▪ HOOKS IN THE CEILING FOR HANGING TRAPEZE, RINGS, OR A SWING. 99

YOU'VE BEEN IN YOUR CAVE TOO LONG WHEN . . .

YOU SEE YOUR CAVE MORE THAN YOU SEE YOUR WIFE. One is your companion for life, your loyal ally, your fountain of comfort, your joy, your bedrock of strength. The other is your wife. Treat her well.

YOU CHOOSE THE CAVE OVER YOUR FRIENDS. A good man cave is one that can be shared with friends. It's not one that *keeps you* from friends. Invite them over; don't freeze them out.

YOU SMELL LIKE FEET. If soldiers could maintain adequate hygiene in the jungles of Korea and the snows of Bastogne, you can find time to change socks and slap on deodorant.

YOU GET A BED. A couch is encouraged. A bed is a slippery slope. Know the difference.

YOU EAT MORE THAN ONE DAILY MEAL IN YOUR CAVE. Zero is best. One is fine. Two is excessive. Three is grounds for divorce in thirty-seven states.

AFTERWORD: IN PROGRESS

Never rush greatness.

It's always darkest before the light. And before a man cave is complete, it will look like post-Katrina New Orleans. This is normal. This is part of the process. No successful project was completed overnight; all the winners take time. (Examples of long-delayed triumphs: Boston's Big Dig, the second Death Star.)

Greatness takes patience. It might take several months until that next jolt of inspiration—should the sofa go on the left wall, or the right wall? You can't rush these decisions.

When your wife says, as patiently as possible, "It's been three years. The garage scares me. It's a safety hazard. I'm embarrassed when the neighbors come by. It smells like animals, and we don't have any pets. When—just level with me, please—when, when, when will this monstrosity be finished?"

You smile, reassure her, hold her hand, hug her, and give her the only answer you can: "Soon."

"I swear, honey,

MY FATHER'S MAN CAVE

My dad never set out to build a man cave.

Yet build one he did. After designing and building a new house when he retired, he finally had something he had coveted for decades: a basement. It was sprawling, empty, unfinished, and, well, cavernous. To the untrained eye, this basement looked drab and dark. To Dad, it had potential. To Dad, it was magical.

He got to work. Inspired, he pored over blueprints, workshop schematics, and wiring diagrams. He built walls. Strung wires for power, audio, and video. Insulated. Hung sheetrock. Installed lights, doors, and finish trim. Painted. He even hooked up plumbing and built a glossy bathroom, complete with shower.

He found space for a computer and study. Room for a treadmill. And he did it all himself. (Okay, he hired a plumber for a day, and a few of us in the family helped with the sheetrock. And while carrying those heavy slabs of evil, I cursed more in two hours than Dad did in two years.)

This wasn't some "hiding place." It was his library, a grown-up sandbox, a place to think and a place to find strength. Before his father, my grandfather, passed away, he bequeathed him a treasure trove of saws, tools, and professional woodworking equipment—this was part of their bond. So Dad built a workshop that would make Grandpa proud. He loved to work, and he worked out of love.

It's still not finished. He still needs to install the dust-collection system, hook up ducts and hoses and God-knows-what-else. But in Dad's words, "The journey has been at least as satisfying as the destination."

THE KEG-O-RATOR

No book about man caves would be complete without instruction on building a keg-o-rator. A triumph of innovation, frugality, and the finer things in life. You can create one yourself. Follow these simple steps from Mike Yost's website, ManCaveSite.org:

1. Inspect the fridge. Be thorough. Scrape away the rotted nacho cheese.

2. Construct a sturdy support base. This will hold your keg and regulator. The existing shelving and a half-inch board will do the trick. If space allows, build a small base from 2x4s and remove bottom shelves.

3. Mark a spot on the inside of the door where you want the faucet to be installed. Using a quarter-inch drill bit, drill a hole all the way through the door. Then drill a 1-3/4-inch hole just through the outside door skin.

4. Does it look like this? Nice work.

5. Drill a 7/8-inch hole over the pilot just through the inside of the door skin.

6. From the outside of the refrigerator, insert the PVC pipe into the door for measurement.

7. Make a cut mark flush with the outside of the door.

8. Hacksaw time! Cut the PVC spacer 1/8-inch shorter than the cut mark you made. Then insert the PVC pipe spacer into the door.

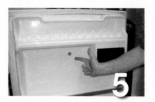

9. Gather all your faucet and shank parts. Attach the knob to the faucet. Tighten.

10. Attach the faucet to the shank as shown. Do not overtighten.

11. Insert shank and faucet into the PVC pipe in the door. Tighten the shank nut on the inside of the door.

12. Check the tightness of the shank and faucet.

13. Does it look like this? Good work. Shank and faucet installed.

14. Add hose clamp (white) over the thin end of the beer hose. Attach the hose to the inside shank fitting. Note: Add moisture to the fitting so the hose will go all the way on.

15. Once on, move the white hose clamp over the fitting. Tighten with pliers until snug.

16. Insert black washer into nut end of beer line. Make a few bad jokes that involve the words "nut end."

17. Screw nut end down onto the coupler. Tighten with a wrench. Chuckle some more about your bad jokes about nut ends being tightened by wenches.

18. Slide hose clamp (white) over the end of the air hose. Hang in there. Almost done.

19. Push the airline over the barbed end of the coupler. Note: Moisten first. Slide clamp over hose and coupler.

20. Tighten air hose clamp. Squeeze firmly to tighten.

21. Put hose clamp over the other end of the air hose.

22. Add air hose and hose clamp. Seriously. Almost done. Mmmmmm, frosty, cold beer. Stay focused.

23. Moisten barbed end of the CO_2 regulator.

24. Attach the air hose to the regulator. Don't do this while drunk.

25. Tighten the hose clamp.

26. Using soapy water, check for leaks on the CO_2 regulator and tank.

27. Check again for leaks.

28. Move bottle and keg into fridge. So close. Almost there. Attach coupler to keg.

29. Does it look like this? Outstanding.

30. A masterpiece.

31. Adjust gauges per the instructions. Pour yourself thirty-one beers, one for each step. Enjoy.

ACKNOWLEDGMENTS

Thanks to my partner in crime, Mike Yost, for welcoming me
into the community with such open arms. His passion, insight, and knowledge about caving is
unparalleled. Mike, the next keg-o-rator's on me.

Huge thanks to editor Matthew Benjamin for being awesome enough (and crazy enough)
to make this happen. Matthew didn't just kick-start the project, he went above and beyond to
shape it, sharpen it, and somehow create order out of the chaos. Thanks to editor Stephanie
Meyers—the closer—for the clutch late-inning pitching. Thanks to hands-down the best (and
nicest) agent in the world, Rob Weisbach, for all the encouragement and support. And thanks
to Trish Daly and Mac Mackie for somehow keeping track of 30 million photographs, and to
designer Timothy Shaner for doing such a kick-ass job with the layout.

To my dad for letting me feature his basement, to my mom for overlooking any lewdness
or profanity (the publisher added that—I swear!), and to all of my friends and family for
putting up with my ramblings about man caves.

To the various experts who had a good enough sense of humor to weigh in on this
important subject: Rachel Hardage, Danny Dumas, Danny Seo, and Dr. Scott Haltzman.

And finally—I can't stress this enough—thanks to all the cavers at ManCaveSite.org.
You guys rock.   —Jeff Wilser

This book would not have been possible without the amazing community on mancavesite.org. You guys are the best. You shared your photos, your stories, and your caves with a bunch of complete strangers. Without you, this book would have just been a bunch of drawings, and it would have sucked. Thank you. Cave on!

Special thanks to the heroes who have caves featured in this book:

Henry Acosta
Cody Babbitt
Greg Battleson
Kerry Beckmann
Glen Bednarczyk
Bob from Michigan
Joe Bottieri
John Bryant
Robby Bryant
Robert Butterfield
Warren Calvert
Cary of Sacramento
R. C. Cavaletto
Steve Clark
Andrew Crout-Hamel
Mark Day
Craig Dayton
Dan Dixon
Richard Dixon
Dr. Zarkov
Lucas Duda

Mike Dunlap
Eric (Gazoo) Faccio
Shawn Floyd
Bob Footitt
Bob Gabaldon
Tony Gallo
Mike Glover
Richard Gooch
Alex Gross
J. C. Hacketts
Jeff Hardy
James Hataway
Eric Hatton
Gary Holder
Josh Holman
Teddy Johnson
Daryl Junge
Troy Kilborn
Jeff Kish
Bill Kurak
Mark Lau

Rob Lee
Roger Lopez
Scott Malandrone
George May
Jim Meehan
Wade Miller
Stephen Mullin
Mike Olson
Billy Osborne
Barry Parkinson
Marty Peterson
Mike Petinarelis
Wyatt Poindexter
Joseph Polisar
Greg (Bubba) Raser
Tim Reveles
Andrew Rocha
Stephen Rose
Cary Ross
Ryan Samuel
Bobby Schaff

John Schmaeling
George Schneider
Jim Schorn
Craig Schuelke
Keith Seminerio
Jeff Smith
Leighton Smith
Chuck Snider
Jason Stanley
Dave Stanoszek
Charles Stayton
Brad Stewart
Joe Stoddard
Mark Sturtevant
Randy Wade
Bill Walker
Alfred Wasilewski
Jon Wilmot
John Young
Waldo Young

ABOUT THE AUTHORS

Jeff Wilser is a nationally-syndicated writer and the author of *The Maxims of Manhood: 100 Rules Every Real Man Must Live By*. His writing has appeared in print or online in *GQ*, *Esquire*, *VH1*, *MTV*, the *Los Angeles Times*, the *Chicago Tribune*, and his trashcan. He is the founding editor of ThePlunge.com and has been called a "relationship expert," although ex-girlfriends would disagree. He lives in New York City, where caves are small and overpriced. He's (grudgingly) on Twitter at @JeffWilser.

Mike Yost is the creator of ManCaveSite.org. He retired as a Sergeant First Class in the U.S. Army after almost eighteen years of service in the military intelligence field. When he is not busy being a man cave expert, he is an IT consultant. Friday or Saturday nights you can usually find him hanging out in his man cave with all his friends. Remember, women are welcome—they just don't have decorating authority! He lives in Sierra Vista, Arizona.